What If Your Best Friend Were Blue?

by **Vera Kochan**

illustrated by **Viviana Garofoli**

Marshall Cavendish Children

All rights reserved
Marshall Cavendish Corporation
99 White Plains Road, Tarrytown, NY 10591
www.marshallcavendish.us/kids

Pinwheel Books

Library of Congress Cataloging-in-Publication Data
Kochan, Vera.
What if your best friend were blue? / by Vera Kochan ; illustrated
by Viviana Garofoli.—1st Marshall Cavendish Pinwheel bk. ed.
p. cm.
Summary: Demonstrates, in simple text and illustrations, that
what people do and how they act is much more important than
what they look like.
ISBN 978-0-7614-5897-5 (hardcover) 978-0-7614-6077-0 (ebook)
[1. Discrimination—Fiction. 2. Behavior—Fiction. 3. Individuality—
Fiction.] I. Garofoli, Viviana, ill. II. Title.
PZ7.K8154Wh 2011   [E]—dc22   2010022522

The illustrations are rendered in acrylic.
Book design by Vera Soki
Editor: Marilyn Brigham

Printed in China (E)
First Marshall Cavendish Pinwheel Books edition, 2011
10 9 8 7 6 5 4 3 2 1

Marshall Cavendish
Children

Thank you, Mom and Dad. You believe in my dreams and that helps them become a reality. Special thanks to Kassie, my "illustrious" niece. Thanks to my editor, Marilyn Brigham, for giving this book a chance.
                    —V. K.

To Maya, with her beautiful eyes . . .
                    —V. G.

What if your best friend were **blue**?

Even if my best friend were blue,
he'd still play soccer with me.

What if a policewoman were green?

Even if a policewoman were green,
she'd still help me find my mom and dad.

What if your doctor were **yellow**?

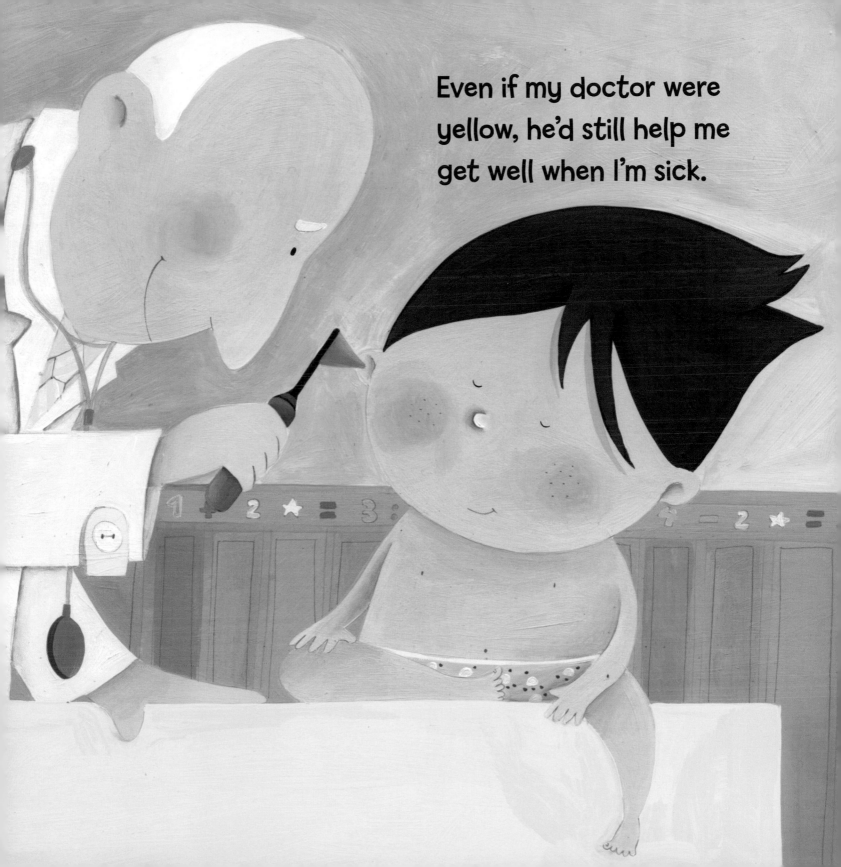

Even if my doctor were yellow, he'd still help me get well when I'm sick.

What if a fireman were **purple**?

Even if a fireman were purple, he'd
still help put out fires around town.

What if your teacher were red?

Even if my teacher were red, she'd still teach me new things each day.

What if your babysitter were **orange**?

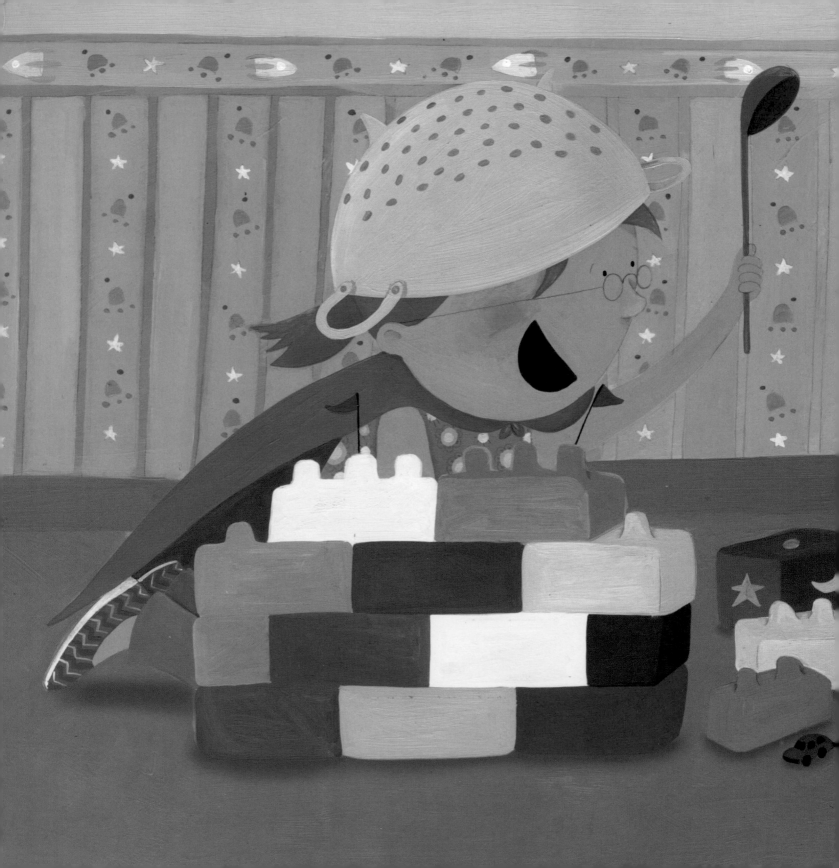

Even if my babysitter were orange, she'd
still think up lots of games for us to play.

And you know what? These people don't care what color you are, either. . . .

They like you just because you're YOU!